Alone in Bellbird Bay

Story by Diana Noonan
Illustrations by Eva Morales

Contents

Chapter 1

Worrying About Grandad

It was Saturday morning, and school holidays were just one week away. Isla was in the kitchen, helping Dad load the dishwasher before the two of them left for archery club. Mum and Ed, Isla's big brother, were filling water bottles to take to their soccer games. But before Mum could put her bottle in her backpack, her phone began to ring.

"It's Grandad," said Mum, peering at the phone's screen as she answered the call. "Hello, Dad," Isla heard Mum say.

"Poor Grandad," said Ed, as Mum walked into the next room with her phone to her ear. "He must be feeling lonely again."

Isla felt sad. Ever since Gran had gone to live in the care home two months ago, Grandad often phoned Mum because he was lonely.

"It will take time for Grandad to get used to not having Gran in the house," said Dad.

But Isla couldn't stop thinking about Grandad, all alone in his little house beside the sea. She looked at the photo of Gran and Grandad on the fridge door. It had been taken before Gran had started forgetting things and getting lost when she went for walks.

When Mum came back into the kitchen a short time later, Isla thought she looked as if she had been crying.

"If only Grandad would join some groups," said Mum in a shaky voice. "Then he would have some company and be much happier."

Isla thought about all the different groups she and her family belonged to, and the friends they made there. During the week, she and Ed went to after-school clubs and drama lessons. Dad went to art class, and Mum went to her photography group. On the weekend, there was archery and soccer.

"Why *won't* Grandad join a group?" Isla asked Mum.

"It can be hard to make changes," said Mum, "especially when you have to do it on your own."

That morning at archery, Isla couldn't get her arrows to hit the target.

"Try to concentrate," Dad encouraged her, but it was no good. Isla just couldn't stop thinking about Grandad being all alone. And she couldn't stop thinking about Gran in the care home, a whole hour's drive away from him.

When Isla and Dad were driving home from archery club, Isla suddenly had an idea that made her feel a little happier. She waited until they got home and everyone was at the table having lunch before she shared it.

"It's school holidays next week," she said, helping herself to one of Mum's famous cheese toastics. "I could go to stay with Grandad to keep him company."

"Don't you want to go to the library holiday program like usual?" asked Mum. "You always look forward to it."

"I *do* like having fun at the library," said Isla, "but this time, I'd rather be with Grandad."

Mum and Dad looked at each other.

"*Please*?" begged Isla.

"Let your dad and me have a think about it," said Mum.

An hour later, when Isla was reading in the living room, Mum appeared with a smile on her face.

"I've just been talking to Grandad again," she said. "He's very much looking forward to having you stay for the first week of the holidays."

Isla jumped up and gave Mum a big hug.

"Thank you," she said. "I can't wait!"

But as Isla went back to reading her book, she started to worry again. She could keep Grandad company for a week, but she couldn't stay with him forever. What would he do for company when she returned home, and he was alone again?

Maybe I can help him join some groups and make new friends, Isla thought.

Chapter 2

Grandad and the Birds

The next Saturday, early in the morning, Dad helped Isla pack her bag to take to Grandad's. Then he carried it out to the car for her. Ed was waiting in the driveway to say goodbye. Mum was already in the driver's seat.

"Have fun at Grandad's," said Dad, opening the car door for Isla.

"Say hi to Grandad from me," said Ed.

Mum backed the car out of the driveway and tooted the horn goodbye. It was a long way to Grandad's, but Mum had packed some sandwiches for lunch.

"We'll call in at Gran's care home on the way," said Mum, "and we can share them with her."

Isla wondered if Gran would remember who she was, but Mum said that even if she didn't, Gran would still enjoy the visit.

At the care home, a woman at reception told Isla and Mum they would find Gran in the lounge. As they made their way there, they could hear the sound of a piano. When they found Gran, she was sitting in a chair, singing happily with some of the other residents.

Gran *did* remember who Isla was, and she smiled when Isla put her arms around her and gave her a big hug.

Mum and Isla joined in the singing, but there was no time to share their sandwiches with Gran afterwards. Gran and her friends from the care home were going to have a picnic in the town's rose garden.

"Do you think Gran misses Grandad?" Isla asked quietly, as they waved Gran off in the care home's minibus.

"I'm sure she does," said Mum. "But she has friends here now, and plenty of activities to take part in. I'm sure that helps."

Isla thought Mum was right. She wished Grandad would make some friends. If he had activities to look forward to, then he would be happier, too, even if he still missed Gran.

It was early afternoon when Mum and Isla finally arrived at the beach. They parked outside Grandad's house. Grandad was sitting on his deck, looking up at the sky through a pair of binoculars. When he saw Isla and Mum, he put the binoculars down and walked across the lawn to meet them.

Isla and Mum got out of the car, and right away, Isla heard a deep droning sound. It was coming from somewhere out at sea.

"It's a search plane," said Grandad after they had greeted each other, when he saw Isla looking over the water.

"A search plane!" said Mum. "Is someone lost?"

"A kayaker has gone missing," said Grandad. "I just heard about it on the radio. A young woman went out fishing in her sea kayak early this morning. She was only going to be away for a couple of hours, but she still hasn't returned."

Isla suddenly spotted a small plane emerging from behind a cloud. It swooped low over the sea.

"But the ocean is so calm," said Mum. "What could have happened to her?"

"A freak wave might have knocked her out of her kayak," said Grandad. "Or she could have hit a reef and got a hole in her boat."

"I hope she's all right," said Isla.

Later that afternoon, Isla and Grandad waved to Mum as she drove away. Then they went into the garden to dig up Grandad's potatoes together. They didn't get much work done, though, because there were so many birds to look at. The birds kept flying into the garden from the forest behind Grandad's house.

"At this time of year, the birds are looking for food to feed their chicks," said Grandad. "Every time we dig up the soil, they see bugs they want to catch."

Isla liked watching the birds. There were so many different kinds, and Grandad knew the names of all of them. Soon, he was teaching her their names.

"Close your eyes and listen hard," said Grandad. "See if you can notice the different calls the birds make."

By the end of the afternoon, Isla knew the names and calls of six different birds.

"All the birds are so pretty," she said to Grandad.

"Yes," said Grandad. "And I like it when they visit me in the garden. They keep me company."

Isla thought Grandad sounded a bit sad when he said that. She wondered if he was thinking about Gran, and how much he missed her.

Chapter 3

Journey to Bellbird Bay

That evening, Grandad cooked dinner and listened to the radio for any news of the missing kayaker. Isla sat at the kitchen table. She was looking at some bird books that Grandad had found for her on his bookshelves.

"Have they found the kayaker yet?" she asked Grandad.

"I'm afraid not," said Grandad. "Let's hope she managed to make it to land and they find her tomorrow morning."

After dinner, Grandad searched the internet for more information about the forest birds he and Isla had seen in the garden. He found some recordings of their songs and played them for Isla, to see if she could recognise them.

"This is fun," said Isla. "I want to know *everything* about the forest birds!"

That was when Grandad made a very exciting suggestion.

"There's a little bay not far from here, where the forest comes right down to the sea," he said. "It's called Bellbird Bay, and there are even *more* kinds of forest birds there. Would you like to visit tomorrow?"

"Yes, please!" said Isla. "How long will it take to drive there?"

"We can't drive there," said Grandad. "There are no roads to Bellbird Bay. We can only get there by boat."

"Will we go in your rowboat?" asked Isla, remembering the little wooden boat Grandad kept in his garage.

"Yes," said Grandad. "We'll pack a picnic and go in the morning."

After breakfast the next morning, Isla and Grandad went out to the garage to get the boat ready for the trip. Isla began thinking about the lost kayaker.

"Will we be safe in our boat on the bay?" she asked Grandad as she put a pair of oars into the boat.

"Yes," said Grandad. "And we're also taking this." He pulled something out of his top pocket that looked a little like a small yellow radio. "It's a Personal Locator Beacon. It's called a 'PLB' for short. There's no mobile phone coverage once we leave the beach, but if we need help in an emergency, I can send a signal on the PLB."

Isla helped Grandad tow the boat on its trailer across the road to the water. Then she and Grandad put on their life jackets.

"There's only just room for us," Isla said as they both got into the boat.

"I built this boat for two people," said Grandad quietly.

Isla was sure Grandad was thinking of Gran, and how they used to go fishing together in the boat.

Grandad picked up the handles of the oars and began rowing. Once the boat was a little way out from shore, he reached into a bag behind him and passed Isla his binoculars.

"It will take us about twenty minutes to reach Bellbird Bay," he said. "See how many different seabirds you can spot on the way, and we can look them up when we get home."

"I will!" said Isla. But just as she was about to start looking, she heard a strange sound.

"That will be a rescue helicopter coming to join the search," said Grandad.

"Why is it taking so long to find the missing kayaker?" Isla asked.

"The sea is a very big place," said Grandad. "And someone lost at sea doesn't just stay in one spot. The tides would keep pushing and pulling them in different directions. A plane or a helicopter could search an area of the ocean and find no one there. But the person they're looking for could float into the area that has just been searched as soon as the rescuers leave."

After Grandad said that, Isla stopped looking through the binoculars for seabirds. Instead, she used them to look out over the water.

Just in case the kayaker is out here, she told herself.

Chapter 4
Isla's Discovery

As Isla scanned the sea, she saw a floating clump of seaweed that looked like a tiny island. She spotted a dark driftwood log bobbing up and down in the water, and a group of black and white seabirds riding the gentle waves. She even spotted a seal poking its nose out of the water not far from the boat.

Grandad rowed and rowed. Soon, the boat had gone around a narrow piece of land and was heading for a long, curved, sandy beach.

"Is that Bellbird Bay?" Isla asked Grandad.

"It is," he told her.

As Grandad rowed towards the beach, Isla raised the binoculars again. But this time, she spotted something that didn't look like it belonged in the sea at all. It was red, and it was floating not very far out from the beach.

Isla wished the object would keep still so she could get a good look at it.

"There's something red out there in the water," she told Grandad as she passed the binoculars to him. "I don't know what it is."

Grandad rested the handles of the oars on his knees and peered through the binoculars.

"It might be a red float that's come loose from a boat," he said. "But we'll row over and check it out."

Isla's heart began to pound. She didn't say anything, but she wondered if the red object might be something to do with the missing kayaker. As Grandad rowed, Isla took back the binoculars and peered through them.

"I think it might be a kayak," she said to Grandad as they drew closer. She passed him the binoculars again. "Would you please take another look, Grandad?"

Grandad put down the oars and looked through the binoculars once more.

"That's *exactly* what it is," he said. "But it's upside down." He began rowing faster. "Good spotting, Isla," he told her.

"We should use your PLB to call for help," said Isla.

"Not yet," said Grandad, puffing. "We may have found the missing kayak, but we don't know if the kayaker is with it. The last thing we want is a rescue helicopter coming all the way here for no reason."

Isla and Grandad were just a few metres away from the kayak when Isla spotted what she thought was a hand. It was holding onto one end of the kayak. When she told Grandad, he began calling out.

"We're coming, we're coming!" he yelled. "Hold on, we're coming for you!"

There was no reply, but now Isla could see the kayaker's fingers. They were moving, but only slightly.

When Grandad had rowed right up to the kayak, Isla saw the young woman. Her head was lying back in the water, and her life jacket was keeping her afloat. Her eyes were closed.

Grandad leaned over the side of the boat and reached for the woman's hand. "We've got you, lass," he said. "You'll be safe soon."

But as soon as Grandad touched the young woman's hand, she panicked. Her fingers gripped his shirt sleeve tightly. Isla couldn't believe the kayaker was still strong enough to do something like that. The woman tugged so hard on Grandad's shirt that she almost pulled him out of the boat.

As Grandad struggled, Isla saw the PLB slip from his pocket. It bumped against the edge of the rowboat and bounced into the sea.

Grandad must have seen it, too, thought Isla, but he didn't say anything. Instead, he stayed calm and pulled himself free from the woman's grip. Then he spoke to her calmly.

"You're going to be okay," he told her. "But I need you to leave your kayak. There's a rope handle on the back of my boat. I want you to hold onto it instead. I can't get you aboard out here, so once you have a hold on the handle, I'm going to tow you to shore. Do you understand?"

The woman gave a low groan, and she closed her eyes again. She let Grandad guide her towards the rear of the boat.

"Good work," Grandad said to the woman as her fingers clasped the rope handle. Then Grandad turned to look at Isla. "Put your hand over hers," he said quietly. "Keep talking to her, and tell me right away if she loses her grip on the rope handle."

Grandad checked behind him, then began rowing carefully.

"We'll be on the beach in ten minutes," he told Isla.

Neither of them said anything about the lost PLB. There was no point.

"That's the way," Isla said to the woman as she floated behind the boat. "You're going to be okay. My grandad knows what to do."

Chapter 5

Alone on the Beach

By the time Grandad had finished rowing to the beach at Bellbird Bay, his brow was covered in sweat.

"Keep hold of the boat so it doesn't float away," Grandad said to Isla as they both hopped out onto the beach.

With Isla's help, Grandad pulled the kayaker into the rowboat. He began rubbing her arms to help warm her up. Her eyes flickered open for a moment, then closed again.

"Bring me my jacket and the water bottle from the bag under the front seat of the boat, please," Grandad said to Isla. But when Grandad put the bottle to the woman's lips, she wasn't able to drink.

"There's no time to lose," said Grandad. "I'm going to row her to the village. That's the fastest way to get her help."

"But we won't all fit in the boat," said Isla. "It's too small for three people."

"I know," said Grandad. Then he looked at Isla very seriously. "I need you to be brave, Isla," he said. "I want you to wait here in Bellbird Bay until I can come back for you."

"Wait all by myself?" asked Isla.

"Yes," said Grandad. "You can do it. I'll only be gone for an hour. While I'm away, I don't want you to go in the water or into the forest. I want you to stay right here on the sand. Can you do that for me?"

Isla looked at the kayaker sitting in the rowboat. She seemed so sick.

"Yes, I can do that," said Isla, as bravely as she could. But she didn't feel brave at all. She felt frightened at the idea of being all by herself in the bay.

"Good girl," said Grandad. "I knew I could rely on you."

Before they left in the boat, Grandad found an extra hat in his bag. He put it on the kayaker's head. "This will help her keep warm when we're out on the water," he said.

"Is she going to be okay?" asked Isla.

But Grandad didn't answer. "Remember to stay on the beach," he said again. "Don't go anywhere else. I'll be back in no time at all."

As Isla watched Grandad row out of the bay and into deeper water, she thought she might cry.

"I have to be brave for Grandad and the kayaker," she said to herself as she held back her tears.

But as Grandad's little boat disappeared around the corner of the bay, Isla felt a tear run down her cheek. She knew another one was on the way.

But before she could wipe her eyes, a little yellow-green bird with a blue tail flew in from the forest. It landed on a piece of driftwood a short distance away. When it opened its beak and called, it sounded exactly like a high-pitched bell. It called again and again. Soon, another bird exactly like it flew in and landed on the same piece of driftwood. Isla took a shaky breath.

"Are you bellbirds?" she asked out loud. "Are you the bellbirds of Bellbird Bay?"

The little yellow-green birds looked right at her. They were close to Isla's feet. She hoped they wouldn't go away.

Chapter 6

An Unexpected Ride

As Isla sat on the sand watching the little birds, the wind began to blow. It sent low waves splashing onto the sand around the bay. It made the trees in the forest behind her rustle and sway.

Isla didn't like the rustling noise. And she didn't like the way the sea was growing more and more choppy. What if a storm was on its way? What if waves splashed into Grandad's boat? What if Grandad's boat tipped over, just like the kayak had?

Isla's face felt hot. She dug her fingers into the sand, but her heart wouldn't stop racing. What if the sea became so rough, Grandad couldn't come back for Isla until tomorrow? What if she had to spend all night alone in the bay, and she had to wait in the dark?

Just when Isla thought she couldn't feel any more frightened, the little yellow-green birds started making their bell calls again. The next minute, a pair of larger birds flew onto the sand beside her. They had stripy black and gold tail feathers. Isla recognised them right away as tiger tails. She had seen them in Grandad's garden the day before. The tiger tails started to sing. The yellow-green birds stopped their single bell chirps and began singing, too.

Before long, more birds from the forest flew onto the beach. Isla knew the names of some of them, but others were new to her. She decided to make up names for the birds she hadn't seen before. She named the tiny birds with tails like fans "fantails". She called the green and brown birds with white tufts at their throats "bow tie birds".

As the wind began to blow harder, some of the forest birds disappeared back into the trees. But now, seabirds were flying in over the white waves. Some landed on the little rocky islands in the bay. Others flew onto the beach and landed a few metres away from Isla. Soon, she was making up names for *them*, too.

Every few minutes, Isla looked out at the water. She wished she could see Grandad rowing back for her. But how could he, now that the sea was so rough?

Just as Isla began to feel afraid again, she heard the sound of a helicopter in the distance. The beat of its propellers grew louder than the wind. A minute later, Isla spotted it. The helicopter was yellow and red, and it was coming from the direction of Grandad's village.

As Isla watched, the helicopter flew right above her, causing the birds to fly away. It dropped lower and lower, then landed on the sand, halfway along the beach. A woman leapt out of the helicopter's cockpit and ducked under the machine's whirring blades. She signalled to Isla to hurry towards her.

Isla stood up and ran across the sand towards the helicopter.

"I'm Jenny," shouted the woman over the noise of the helicopter's blades. "I'm a helicopter pilot. I'm going to take you back to the village in the helicopter. Your grandad is waiting there for us."

"Is the kayaker all right?" shouted Isla.

"Yes," said Jenny, nodding. "An ambulance has taken her to hospital. She's going to be fine."

Jenny helped Isla step up into the helicopter's cockpit, then closed the door behind her. When Jenny was in her pilot seat, she buckled Isla into a safety belt. She put a set of earmuffs on Isla's head, which made the propellers much less noisy.

As Jenny piloted the helicopter up into the sky, Isla looked down on the rough sea. No wonder the kayaker had been hard to spot from the air, she thought. Everything looked so tiny from this height!

Five minutes later, Jenny was landing the helicopter in a field close to Grandad's village. As Isla looked out of the cockpit, she could see Grandad. He was standing beside his car, waving to her.

"Welcome back!" shouted Grandad, as Isla jumped down from the cockpit and ran over to him. "Did you enjoy your ride?"

"It was *amazing*!" said Isla.

Chapter 7

Grandad's Big News

As Grandad drove Isla back to his house, the two of them talked and talked. Grandad told Isla how hard it had been to row against the wind. He told her the kayaker's name was Wai, and that she was only nineteen.

"Wai did very well to keep holding on to her kayak after it overturned," he said.

Isla told Grandad about feeling afraid on the beach, especially when the wind began to blow. She also told him about how worried she had been that he wouldn't be able to come back for her until the next day.

"You were very brave," said Grandad.

That afternoon, Isla phoned Mum and Dad to tell them about everything that had happened.

Later, there was a knock at the door. It was a newspaper reporter named Tim.

He asked if he could come in and talk to Grandad and Isla about finding the kayaker. Grandad said he could.

Tim took a photo of Isla and Grandad sitting together on the sofa.

"Was it scary having to stay at Bellbird Bay all by yourself?" Tim asked Isla.

"It was," she told him. "But there were lots of birds to watch. Seabirds flew in to the bay, and there were lots of forest birds flying around. Some of them even landed very close to my feet and sang to me."

"So, the birds kept you company?" asked Tim.

"They did!" said Isla brightly. "The Bellbird Bay birds kept me company!"

After Tim left, Isla and Grandad didn't talk to anyone else all week. And the only other people they saw were the mail delivery man and a family walking on the beach. At the end of the week, when Mum came to take Isla home, Isla felt sad to be leaving Grandad alone again.

"I wish we could get Grandad to join a group so he could have some company," Isla told Mum on the way home. "He talks to the birds, but it's not like having real friends."

When Isla got back home, there was still a whole week of holidays left. Every afternoon, she went to swimming lessons with her friends from school. As she floated in the water, she thought about Grandad alone in his house, missing Gran in the care home. She thought about him alone in the garden, with no one but the birds to talk to.

By the end of the week, even Mum was beginning to feel concerned about Grandad.

"It's strange that he hasn't called me for several days," she said one night at dinner. "I think I'll call him after we've eaten and see what he's up to."

But right after dinner was finished, Mum's phone started ringing from the living room. Mum went to answer it. She put it on speaker as she came back into the kitchen. It was Grandad!

"I was wondering where you'd got to," Mum said. "We haven't heard from you all week."

"Oh," said Grandad, "that's because I've been busy."

"Oh, really?" asked Mum. "Busy doing what?"

"I've joined our village birdwatching group," Grandad said.

Isla was helping Dad and Ed with the dishes. She nearly dropped a glass in surprise.

"I see," said Mum calmly, as she looked up at everyone with a small smile.

"There's just seven of us in the group," continued Grandad. "But we're hoping to get new members. So far, we go birdwatching on Wednesdays, and we have our actual meeting on Saturday afternoons."

Now Mum was grinning widely.

"Some of the members go to a walking group on Monday mornings," said Grandad. "So I might join them."

Isla was nearly jumping up and down with happiness.

"Of course, none of it makes up for not having Gran here," he said. "But I can't keep being a hermit. When Isla came to stay, I remembered how good it was to have someone to talk to. So, I thought, why not join a group and meet a few people?"

Mum nodded as she looked at Isla, Ed and Dad, who were all listening intently.

"Great idea, Dad," she said into the phone.

Mum started to say something else, but Grandad said he had to go. "A man from my birdwatching group is calling in later to borrow one of my bird books," he said. "I'd better go and find it before he arrives."

After Mum had hung up, everyone in the kitchen began clapping.

"Well done, Isla!" said Mum.

"Now Grandad has birds *and* friends for company," said Ed.

"Yes," said Dad. "Going to stay with Grandad was a great idea!"

"And he can tell Gran all about it when he visits her on Sundays!" said Isla. "It's *perfect*!"